MORE SPECIAL O~~FFERS~~
FOR MR MEN AND LITTLE ~~MISS~~

D0806419

In every Mr Men and Little Miss book like thi~~s~~
sticker and activity books, you will find a special~~~~
will send you a gift of yo~~ur~~
Choose either a <u>Mr Men</u> or <u>Little Miss</u> poster, **or** a Mr Men or Little Miss
double sided full colour bedroom door hanger.

Return this page **with six tokens per gift required** to:

> Marketing Dept., MM / LM, World International Ltd.,
> PO Box 7, Manchester, M19 2HD

Your name:_____ Age: _____

Address: _____

_____

_____Postcode: _____

Parent / Guardian Name (Please Print)_____

Please tape a 20p coin to your request to cover part post and package cost

I enclose <u>six</u> tokens per gift, and 20p please send me:-

<u>Posters:-</u>	Mr Men Poster ☐	Little Miss Poster ☐
<u>Door Hangers</u> -	Mr Nosey / Muddle ☐	Mr Greedy / Lazy ☐
	Mr Tickle / Grumpy ☐	Mr Slow / Busy ☐
20p	Mr Messy / Quiet ☐	Mr Perfect / Forgetful ☐
	L Miss Fun / Late ☐	L Miss Helpful / Tidy ☐
	L Miss Busy / Brainy ☐	L Miss Star / Fun ☐

Please Tick Appropriate Box

Stick 20p here please

We may occasionally wish to advise you of other Mr Men gifts.
If you would rather we didn't please tick this box ☐

ENTRANCE FEE
3 SAUSAGES

MR. GREEDY

|— 100 mm —|

250 mm

Collect six of these tokens
You will find one inside every
Mr Men and Little Miss book
which has this special offer.

1
TOKEN

Offer open to residents of UK, Channel Isles and Ireland only

Full colour Mr Men and Little Miss Library Presentation Cases in durable, wipe clean plastic.

In response to the many thousands of requests for the above, we are delighted to advise that these are now available direct from ourselves, for only **£4.99** (inc VAT) plus 50p p&p.
The full colour boxes accommodate each complete library. They have an integral carrying handle as well as a neat stay closed fastener.
Please do not send cash in the post. Cheques should be made payable to **World International Ltd. for the sum of £5.49** (inc p&p) per box.

Please note books are not included.

Please return this page with your cheque, stating below which presentation box you would like, to:-
Mr Men Office, World International
PO Box 7, Manchester, M19 2HD

Your name:_____

Address: _____

_____

_____Postcode: _____

Name of Parent/Guardian (please print):_____

Signature:_____

I enclose a cheque for £_____ made payable to World International Ltd.,

Please send me a Mr Men Presentation Box ☐

    Little Miss Presentation Box ☐   (please tick or write in quantity) and allow 28 days for delivery

Thank you

Offer applies to UK, Eire & Channel Isles only

little Miss Curious

by Roger Hargreaves

WORLD INTERNATIONAL

Little Miss Curious is a very curious
sort of person.

Just look at her house.

It's a very curious shape.

Isn't it?

"Why do flowers live in beds but never sleep?" she asked the flowers in her garden.

They just smiled, knowingly.

Then she saw a worm.
"Why do worms in Nonsenseland wear bow-ties?" she asked.

"That's for me to know and you to find out about," said the worm, laughing.

we look

Later, on the way to town,
Little Miss Curious met
Mr Nonsense.

Are you curious to find out
what she asked him?

Well go on then, turn over!

"I'm curious … " began Little Miss Curious,
" … to know why it is that sandwiches
are called sandwiches if they don't have
any sand in them."

"It just so happens," said Mr Nonsense,
"that this is a **sand** sandwich. I'm
rather partial to sand!"

"Happy Christmas," he said.

Then Mr Nonsense ran away holding his sandwich carefully so that the sand didn't fall out.

Little Miss Curious eventually arrived
in town.

Did I hear you ask, "Why?"

Well, you are curious,
aren't you?

But are you as curious as
Little Miss Curious?

Little Miss Curious had gone to
town to visit the library.

"I wonder, would you be able to
help me?" she asked

"Of course," said Mrs Page, the librarian.
"What are you looking for?"

"I'm looking for a book," began
Little Miss Curious,
"a book that will tell me
why the sky is blue … "

" ... and why combs have teeth,
but can't bite,
... and why chairs have legs,
but can't play football,
... and why ... "

And she went on,
and on,
and on,
until there was a very long queue
behind her, that was growing longer
by the minute.

"That's enough!" cried Mrs Page.

"NEXT PLEASE!"

"But why … " Little Miss Curious started to ask.

But without quite knowing how or why,
she suddenly found herself out in the street.

"How curious," Little Miss Curious
thought to herself.

As she walked along the street,
Little Miss Curious asked herself:
"Why is everybody giving me
such curious looks?
And why is Little Miss Careful waving
her umbrella at me?
Is it because it's going to rain?"

We don't think so, do we?

Little Miss Curious ran off.

Are you going to ask, "Why?"

Are you becoming as curious as
Little Miss Curious?

Can you guess
where she ran off to?

Neither can I.

Come back Little Miss Curious
and tell us where you're going!

You see, we're all ever so curious.

Yes, really we are!